The Urbana Free Library

To renew: call **217-367-4057**
or go to **urbanafreelibrary.org**
and select **My Account**

The Rotary Club of Urbana is
pleased to donate this book to
The Urbana Free Library
in honor of:

Janice McAteer
DSC

Sometimes Even Elephants Forget

Written by
Kathleen Welch

Illustrated by
Alan McGillivray

A Story About Alzheimer's Disease for Young Children

PELICAN PUBLISHING COMPANY

GRETNA 2019

Library of Congress Cataloging-in-Publication Data

Names: Welch, Kathleen, 1956- author. | McGillivray, Alan, illustrator.
Title: Sometimes even elephants forget : a story about Alzheimer's Disease for young children / written by Kathleen Welch and illustrated by Alan McGillivray.
Description: Gretna : Pelican Publishing Company, 2019. | Summary: Grandma Bawa needs help from her grandson, Mookie, and a friend when she gets lost in Jala Jungle, but when a lion threatens the elephant herd, she remembers how to sound the alarm.
Identifiers: LCCN 2018028282 | ISBN 9781455624690 (hardcover : alk. paper) | ISBN 9781455624706 (ebook)
Subjects: | CYAC: Memory—Fiction. | Grandmothers--Fiction. | Alzheimer's disease—Fiction. | Elephants--Fiction. | Jungles—Fiction.
Classification: LCC PZ7.1.W43513 Som 2019 | DDC [E]—dc23
LC record available at https://lccn.loc.gov/2018028282

Printed in Malaysia
Published by Pelican Publishing Company, Inc.
1000 Burmaster Street, Gretna, Louisiana 70053
www.pelicanpub.com

Once upon a tropical time in the exotic Jala Jungle
lived a jolly elephant family who loved to wear purple.
They wore purple hats. They wore purple caps. They
wore purple skirts. They wore purple shirts.

Like any elephant family, there were some wise
leaders. Grandma Bawa was one of the wise leaders.
She took care of all the little ones. Her nimble trunk
was like her right hand. It was very helpful in taking
care of the children.

One morning, she unwound her long trunk to gently nudge her grandson, Mookie, awake.

"Rise and shine, sleepy head!"

Mookie wobbled a bit when he stood up. Grandma Bawa saw he was ready for the day. He had slept in his sporty shorts and cap! It was the first day of summer vacation. Mookie wanted to play from the minute he woke up.

On his way to kiss Grandma Bawa, he looked up and
noticed that something was different.

"Grandma, where is your purple hat? You always
wear your favorite hat."

"Oh, dear! I don't remember where I put it, Wasu. I do
like my sun hat. Your Grandpa Bawa just bought it for
me yesterday at the flea market."

"We'll find it," said Mookie.

They looked on the thorny tree hat rack. Not there.
Mookie saw it on a nearby rock.

"Here it is," said Mookie. He knew that Grandma
Bawa sometimes forgot his name and that Grandpa
Bawa had died a long time ago. He didn't correct
Grandma Bawa because she was forgetting things. He
knew she still loved him all the same.

Mookie was ready to go have some fun!
"Grandma, can you show me the way to the
Rumba River? We can go splash, play and cool
off!"

"Just hook up your trunk to my tail and away
we go."

Grandma Bawa led the way. She liked to tell family stories. She told Mookie about Grandpa Bawa buying the beautiful hat at the flea market. Grandma Bawa liked that story. She would tell it many times. Mookie didn't mind. He knew that the story made her feel happy.

"Grandma, look at our footprints! I think we are going in circles. I think we're lost!"

Grandma Bawa was very upset. She had known the way to the river only last week. Now she couldn't remember.

Luckily, they ran into Kip, the clever hedgehog. They asked him the way. Kip was not only clever. He was also kind. "Don't worry, Grandma Bawa, you are here and that's all that matters. I'll be happy to show you the way. I'm hot, too."

Kip jumped onto Grandma
Bawa's trunk and pointed the way.

They reached the river in no time. Grandma Bawa,
Mookie and Kip started to play and bathe. Grandma Bawa
always had her special brush for bathing, but not this
time.

"I forgot my lion whisker brush!"

"That's OK," said Kip. "I have a fine natural brush. Me!"

Mookie wanted to help, too. "Grandma, I'll spray you with my trunk!"

Even the jungle butterflies helped Grandma
Bawa bathe. They softly fluttered over her eyes to
shield her from the water and the glare of the sun.

Splish, splash! So much fun!

Then everything changed. A lion roared!
The jungle shook! Birds screeched! Fish
jumped! Mookie screamed, "Grandma, save
us! It's a lion!"

They needed to act fast. All three waded
farther into the river, away from the lion.

They were safe! Then the lion started to slink
towards the home of their elephant family.

Mookie knew they had to help their family right away! "Grandma, can you remember the ancient call to warn our family?"

She thought and wrinkled her brow. "Yes! I can. I still remember some things from long ago. I'll do the Honk Wonk Stomp Whomp! That will alert our family that a lion is on the prowl."

She made three loud honks.

She made three startling wonks.

She made three rumbling stomps.

Then she made three low whomps.

The elephant family heard the Honk Wonk Stomp
Whomp through the air and through their feet! The
family did what they always do when there is a threat.
They quickly huddled together and fled.

The lion was too lazy to run after the elephants. He
slinked away into the jungle instead!

Grandma Bawa was still very worried about the family. "Mookie and I better go check on our family. We need to see if they heard the Honk Wonk Stomp Whomp."

"That sounds like a good idea," Kip squeaked. "I better be going too. I'm late for a very important date with my sweetheart!"

When Grandma Bawa bent down to kiss Kip goodbye, her lion whisker brush fell out of her skirt pocket. "I thought I lost that."

"I can put my lion whisker brush to good use now. Let me brush you so you razzle dazzle your girlfriend!" She forgot which side of the brush to use but Kip didn't care. His silver quills quivered in delight. He was too excited about his date. He squealed, "I will razzle dazzle her now! Will you two be all right after I leave?"

Grandma Bawa answered, "Sure, we'll be fine."
"Goodbye! Goodbye!" they squeaked and tooted.
Kip went in one direction and Mookie and Grandma
Bawa in the other. Grandma Bawa led for several miles.
She started going in circles. This time Mookie came to
the rescue. He trotted in front of her to show her the way.
"Grandma, we can follow our footprints all the way back
to our family. Grab my tail with your trunk!"

When Grandma Bawa and Mookie arrived home, the very happy elephant family threw a honky tonk party! "Thank you, Grandma Bawa. We heard your Honk Wonk Stomp Whomp and knew what to do!" cheered the family. "You saved us! You are queen for the day! Here is your crown."

Grandma Bawa smiled. She tried to put the crown on one of her floppy ears instead of her head.

"It doesn't matter where you wear the crown,"
said the family. "You are here and that's all that
matters." Mookie then helped her put the crown on
her head. "We love you, Grandma!"

Now it was time to celebrate and dance the Honk Tonk
Rump Bump! Big and little elephant rumps bumped!

Even Kip heard the celebration and rumped
bumped with his sweetheart. The jungle shook in joy
and happiness. It was a real honky tonk party!

Furthering the Conversation

Older people and elephants can forget and get mixed up. In this story, that happens to Grandma Bawa.

Your grandma or grandpa may forget what they once knew. They may also repeat things and make up stories. This can make things hard for everyone. Sometimes this is caused by Alzheimer's. This disease affects millions of people.

You can be like Mookie. Listen to your grandma or grandpa with loving kindness. They still love you. It's just that their brain isn't working as well as it once did.

Be patient and listen to them. It's OK if they make a mistake talking to you. Try not to interrupt and correct them. Most of all make them feel important and loved. And always try to treasure the good times you had with them.

Facts and Resources

Alzheimer's is a medical disorder of the brain that slowly destroys the cells responsible for memory and thinking. It is not a normal part of the aging process. People over sixty are most at risk.

Alzheimer's is a devastating disease, which affects over five million Americans. It is the only disease of the top ten leading causes of death where there is no prevention or cure.

This book can be used as a way to discuss the disease with your child or loved one if someone you know has Alzheimer's. You can talk to them about some of the symptoms, which Grandma Bawa shows, such as short-term memory loss, getting lost, telling the same story repeatedly, an inability to complete simple routine tasks, and not recognizing loved ones.

Mookie provides an excellent example of how a child can respond to someone with Alzheimer's. You can tell your child that the person with Alzheimer's loves you but sometimes has trouble remembering just like Grandma Bawa. When this happens, it is best to act like Mookie and not get upset. Instead help and reassure them that you love them.

Here are some other great resources on helping children and teens interact with someone who has Alzheimer's:

Alzheimer's Association: https://www.alz.org/documents/national/brochure_childrenteens.pdf

Fisher Center for Alzheimer's Research Foundation: https://www.alzinfo.org